2020. 10. 9

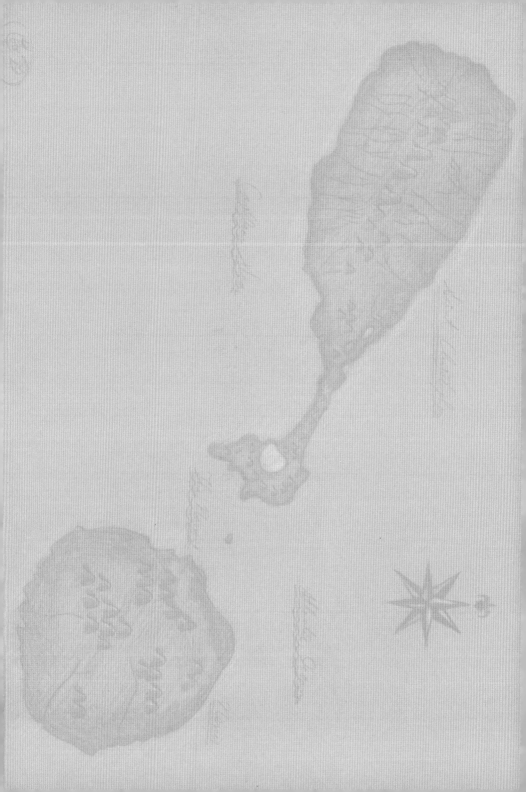

航向驚嘆島

Sailing to
the Islands of Exclamation

望海甘比
Gambi and Seas

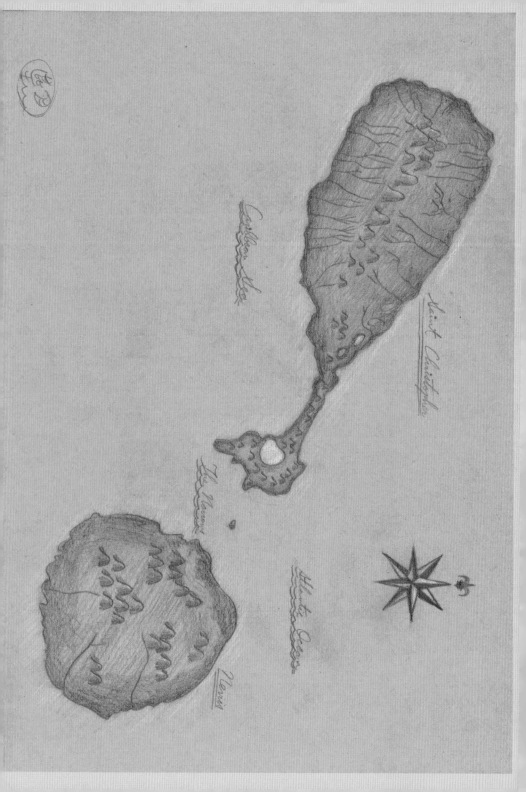

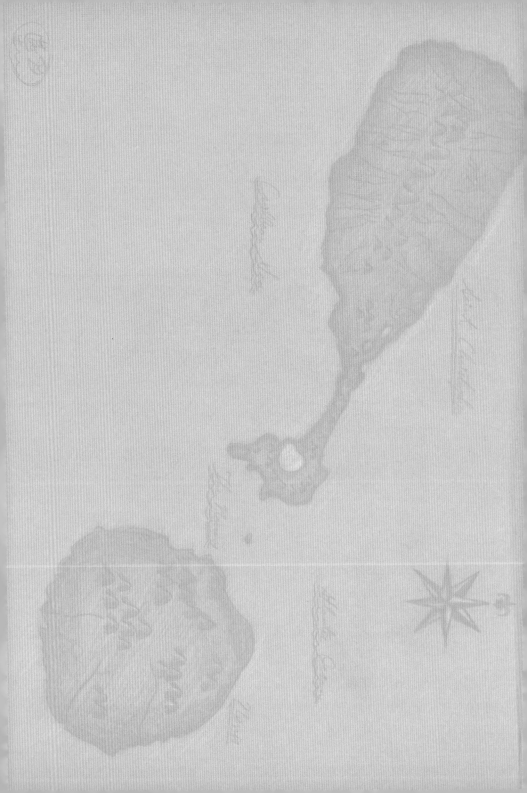

目錄 Contents
自序 Preface
誌謝 Acknowledgement

自序

　　這是關於一位旅者及流浪者誕生的敘事詩。

自大航海時代開始，長途探索一直都是個極為耗費金錢的投資，而這些經歷換來新穎辛香料的可能及自然史的拼貼畫，也就此拓展探險者們、讀者們及資助者的眼界。在「航向驚嘆島」中被提及的驚嘆島，就外型而言它確實存在，即為聖克里斯多福及尼維斯。它是世界上的袖珍型國家之一（世界第八小的國家），位於加勒比海背風群島與向風群島的會合點。就意義上而言，驚嘆島就是資助者給予他的一個探索機會，從那裡尋找自我、拓展他自己本身眼界，亦帶給讀者不同的視野。

「航向驚嘆島」一書的原型是100封明信片上的極短詩，也就是說手稿四散在100人手中（有些可能早已海上迷途）。當他抵達此島，他的朋友與家人們甚是驚喜，便開始向他索取明信片。當時的他思索著如何將問候與創作同時寫在篇幅甚小的明信片上，此時他想起松尾芭蕉「奧之細道」中的俳句（世界最小的文體），正好適合明信片的篇幅，最後決定以三行詩的方式記錄他在這裡的所見所聞及虛實狂想。除了形式上的問候，他讓朋友們依照他們喜好定下主題，讓他戴著腳鐐跳舞，並附上幾幅在此地所繪的色鉛筆素描畫，像是著名觀光景點巴克禮鐘塔（原蘇格蘭格拉斯哥鐘塔的復刻版）、硫磺山要塞（1999年入選世界文化遺產）等。

在「航向驚嘆島」中，詩不再只是種古典、嚴謹的姿態。除了對當地歷史人文之嚴肅追憶及詠嘆，他亦使用簡單的日常用語敘事、詩頌生活，又如頑童般運用科學、奇幻、偽科學名詞另闢新的境地，營造出一種他與自我或他人的靈魂對話氛圍。那些敘述簡單的日常用語及對話本身毫無規則可循，而他在此便添加一個以6的因數為基礎的分段規則（英譯版沒有此規則）呈現日常用語的極簡模樣。此外，文中提到的一些生態學、物理學的名詞或許會讓守舊派的詩人會有些反感。然而若歌詞也是種詩體，在現今一些歌曲靈感確實來自生物學、環境保護議題（如Nightwish的The Greatest Show On Earth、Epica的This Is The Time），甚至是

近代物理學（如Epica的Holographical Principle）。或許就像這些樂團的作詞者，他們只是一位引路人，在一棟詩的城堡裡，藉由這些詞創造通往多個隱藏房間的門，讀者的認知是把可塑的鑰匙，越有共鳴的讀者能開啟越深層的隱藏房間，使這些被既定的專有名詞在詩的世界也有了亞交流的可能。舉例來說，用「自組裝」的概念闡釋那未被殖民的時空；用生態學的「綠世界假說」重新詮釋拉斯塔法里教徒的心境；「對流浪的渴望」一詩以熵來形容每個故事的誕生過程等。另一方面，部分詩中也融入一些奇幻及在學術界被視為禁忌的元素，如「艾瑪芮思」、「蒸氣龐克時空」及「水猿」等，它們在詩的世界中得到解放。

原本他著墨至此便準備要出版了，卻有個巨大的轉變。這裡有個英譯的故事，也就是為何自己書寫雙語詩？畢竟「航向驚嘆島」本身並非華語地區的產物，而是來自地球另一端的世界，除了華語地區，來自世界各地的旅者都有可能對此感到好奇。他在驚嘆島的酒吧與一位詩人朋友相遇，為了紀念這段奇遇，他寄了一封附上中文詩創作的明信片給了這位詩人。當她收到時卻深感可惜，因為看不懂中文，他連忙附上英譯版給她，起碼讓她了解他詩的含義。因為這個緣故讓他下定決心，即便英文的表達能力與語韻安排的能力仍有限，也要盡全力詮釋自己原詩的意境。不禁感嘆在巴別塔之後許多語言誕生，世界市民間出現了隔閡。幸好現今還有英文能普遍將各地旅者及流浪者連結起來，巨大世界中渺小的旅者／流浪者如他無法一一翻譯每個語言，至少做點英文翻譯，讓世界市民及旅者／流浪者得知這裡也有個剛問世的流浪者在此如新生兒般大哭、大笑。

這是個旅者及流浪者充斥的時代，而每個人內心都有著一座自己「驚嘆島」，等待著一個自我的「引爆」或幸運地得到「資助」，這座島即是一個讓人們認知靠岸、靈魂甦生的地方。

Preface

This is a descriptive poetry about the birth of a traveler, or a wanderer.

Since the Discovery Age, voyages have been always upscale investments. However, these experiences became the possibility of cutting-edge spices and the collages of natural history. Namely, these investigations have truly broadened the horizons of the discoverers, readers and sponsors. The islands in 'Sailing to the Islands of Exclamation' is indeed exist in terms of the shape, it is Saint Christopher and Nevis, which is one of mini-country in the world (The eighth one of the smallest country in the world). It is at the boundary of Leeward Islands and Windward Islands. In addition, in terms of the meaning, the islands symbol an opportunity of discovery granted by sponsors. Also, it made him discover himself and broaden his and readers' horizons.

'Sailing to the Islands of Exclamation' actually originated from 100 Haiku-like poems on postcards; namely, the manuscripts are now in 100 people's places respectively (despite that some ones were missed already). When he arrived the islands, his friends and family members were surprised and therefore asked for local postcards. He considered how to put his greetings and writings together on such limited space of each postcard. Then, he recalled the Haiku (The shortest poem in the world) from 'Bashos Narrow Road to a Far Province' of Matsuo Basho. Finally, he decided to use this form to record what he saw and what he thought in reality or fantasy. Besides the formal greetings, he let friends decided the topics of poems so that he could be a dancer with shackles. Also, he drew the illustrations, such as the scenic spots Berkeley Memorial (the duplicate of the clock tower in Glasgow,

Scotland), Brimstone Hill Fortress (UNESCO World Heritage Site since 1999), by colour pencil.

In 'Sailing to Island of Exclamation', the poems here are not classical and critical anymore. Besides the recalling and sighing for the local history and culture of Caribbean, he also used simple and colloquial words to describe scores of things and the life here. Also, as a naughty boy, he has used such words only in sciences, fantasy, and pseudoscience to construct the extra rooms of his poetry; subsequently, concerning the conversations between his own soul and someone else, a refreshing atmosphere was created. There is no rule about these simple words and conversations, while he created a rule that can separate the sentences by the divisors of 6 (There is no the rule in English version) to present extremely simple daily conversations. In addition, such words about ecology and physics probably make the conservative poets annoyed, yet, if lyrics belong a genre of poem, the lyrics of some songs indeed inspired from biology, environmental science ('The Greatest Show On Earth' of Nightwish, 'This Is The Time' of Epica) and, even, modern physics ('Holographical Principle' of Epica). Perhaps, as the songwriters of these bands, he is just a guide man in this castle of poetry. The doors to the hidden rooms are created with these words; besides, the readers' background knowledge are flexible keys. More senses the readers have, deeper rooms they discover. Therefore, within the world of the poetry, it is possible that the sub-communications of these defined words happen. For instance, 'Self-assembly' was used to explain the time and space without colony; The mind of Rasta men/women were reflected by 'Green World Hypothesis', which originates from Ecology; The 'entropy' mentioned in 'Wanderlust' was used to describe the process of the birth of each story. On the other hand, a part of poems was added with the elements of fantasy and what are strongly forbidden in academy, such as 'Amaranth', 'the time and space of steampunk', 'Water Ape' and so on; however, in this poetic world, they have been liberated. He was going to publish this poetry, yet there was a huge change. That is to say, why did he write a bilingual poetry? After all, 'Sailing to the Islands of Exclamation' is totally not from the areas filled with Chinese speakers, it is from the other side of the Earth. Besides the Eastern Asia, the travelers worldwide are probably curious about it. He met a poet friend in a bar, and he sent a postcard to her to commemorate their serendipity. However, she felt pity because she doesn't understand Chinese. He therefore sent the message which the English version of the poem was enclosed to her. At least, she could understand the meaning. That is the reason why he decided to and try his best to write a bilingual poetry despite of his limited expression and control of rhythms. Hence, He could not help but sigh, there are gaps amongst the citizens of the world after the event named Babel Tower. Fortunately, English is the language which can commonly connect with the travelers and wanderers worldwide. He, as grain traveler and wanderer, in the tremendous world cannot do the translation for every single language but English. At least, it can let the traveling and wandering people realize that there is a birth of a wanderer, and he cries, or laughs, like a newborn. This is the age with numerous travelers and wanderers. Everyone has his/her own 'Islands of Exclamation'. They are waiting for an 'explosion' by himself/herself or, luckily, 'sponsors'. Then, the islands are where their awareness arrive and where their souls revive.

誌謝

首先向國際合作發展基金會致上最誠摯的感謝，讓敝人有此機會外派至聖克里斯多福及尼維斯生活，也感謝提供敝人明信片主題的100位朋友及家人們。特別感謝駐地計畫經理、技師、志工與語訓老師等人的照顧。感謝思萍、薏婷、詠喬及怡誼等人在新詩用字遣詞、當地歷史引用上的指正及勘誤。最後，感謝Zeida Montero在英譯版文法的指正、Jessica Rivas及강지혜在英譯版上的試閱！

Acknowledgement

At first, I highly appreciate Taiwan International Cooperation Development Fund for the opportunity to live in St. Kitts and Nevis. I also appreciate the cares of the project managers and technicians, volunteers, our language teacher, etc. In addition, I highly thank for Spring, Tina, Chiau, Yiyi and so on for the suggestions and corrections on word play and local history. Finally, about the English version, I truly appreciate the grammatical help from my friend Zeida Montero and the reviews of Jessica Rivas and Jihye Kang.

零與靈
Zero 'n' Soul

I.

「你該習慣都市，還有穩定法則！」
「我，忍著，再忍著……
「他媽的，我究竟，還能追求什麼？」

寂靜的你創造自喧囂的城，
城的喧囂卻引爆你的乖戾，
乖戾的你轉動起城的旅行。

-即時旅者-

'You are supposed to adapt to city life and the rules!'
'I…adapted to it and adapted it…'
'Damn, what do I search for actually?'

A tranquil you are from a noisy city,
Yet the noise from the city ignites a grumpy you,
The you are rolling the traveling of the city.

-Immediate Traveler-

II.

「你記得，忘掉所有成見，接納一切所見。」

含記憶的酒杯，
為了裝滿新酒，
要再洗一次杯。

-探索前-

'Please remember, forget everything in your mind and accept
all you see.'

A Glass with memory,
To pour new wine into,
Wash anew fully

-Before Exploring-

巴士底

Basseterre

III.

「你現在在哪了？我很好。

「但⋯我想，如神像，除了回憶河流，不會再見了吧⋯」

我將你的神像拿去典當，

愛慾及靈魂週轉，怕窮的心

使你在我一生中流當。

-關於你的神像-

'Where are you now? I'm good.

'But⋯I think, just like the statue, I won't see you again except

as a river of memory⋯'

I have stolen your statue for a pawn,

Turnover of my desire and soul, that fear from poverty

Let you flow into the river of my life.

-About Your Statue-

IV.

聖克里斯多福、尼維斯，首都是巴士底。法文中的「低地」。在
大航海時代，先被法國佔領，再被英國佔領。

他離去我的國度，故事在土地上。
今日街景和交談沿用著你的語言，
首都，仍以舊日異國之名流芳。

-追憶巴士底-

Saint Christopher and Nevis. The capital is Basseterre, which

means 'low land' in French. In the Age of Discovery, here was

first occupied by French, and then occupied by British.

Her leaving from my hand, the story of the land.

On the street, your language is still in the mouths of today;

In the capital, they still use your exotic name.

-Recalling for Basseterre-

V.

穿越光之門，
多方文明倒影震碎了眼睛。
渺小時刻，重組胸襟。

-穿越桑提耶-

Going across the bright gate,

My eyes are shattered by reflections of civilizations.

As grain as me, re-construction of my gate.

-Going across Port Zante-

VI.

「敬！你我，又是一日終焉！」

千百艘郵輪來去我的暮朝。
一日終焉，向淌金淚的海靈進酒，
任郵輪們的筆跡就此雲消。

-守島人-

'Bottom-up, you and me finished a day again!'

Thousands of ships pass by my dusk and dawn.

At the end of each day, bottoms up with the sob ocean,

And erase the tracks of ships as passing clouds.

-The Islander-

VII.

凝視蘇格蘭的今昔之眼，
由朝聖者、流浪的住民共同
見證死亡與存活的時間。

-失落的鐘塔-

I gaze at the historic eye of Scotland,

Let the pilgrims and wandering citizens

Be the witnesses of dying and alive time.

-Faded Campanile-

Berkeley Memorial
Griffith

VIII.

敬邀世界各地的樹人見證，
來自雨林深處、東亞和換雪的地方，
為這美麗的土地引來自由之風。

-詠獨立廣場-

Let's invite the ents worldwide,
From rainforests, eastern Asia, and wherever with periodic snows,
Bring the wind of freedom for the Land of Beauty.

-Singing for Independence Square-

IX.

當夏天走向永恆，
日子遲鈍，且莽原緩慢，
褪色的花也捨棄凋零。

-艾瑪芮思-

When Summer is being eternal,

Days delayed, and the savanna is slowed;

Fading flowers also gives up withering.

-Amaranth-

Amaranth

X.

鵜鶘，國鳥？

掠過水面、短暫漂泊
群聚地方的海灘，而遠飛者
常以家鄉魚腥拜訪漁火

-鵜鶘-

They pass, short-term stay on waves

Or commute on a beach, but the roving ones

Visit fishermen's boats with the taste of home

-Pelicans-

XI.

多米尼克及克國；農產品進口商、習慣的中間商。

它與它來自多米尼克的墳上
熟悉的浪頭打在市集旁的粗放海灘
被遺忘、被唾棄，我曾耕作的土壤

-廢耕者-

Dominica and St. Kitts & Nevis; the importer and middleman of
agriculture products.

It and it are from the grave in Dominica
Familiar waves reach the long beach near the market
The forgotten, ignored soil was once in my farm

-Forgotten Farmers-

XII.

「那裡有炸雞店。」
「哪裡？那民宅？」

告訴每位飢餓的熟客：
僅限小額交易、快速簡單的餐盒
每當窗子闔上──一間房舍

-一扇窗口-

'There is a fried-chicken vendor.'
'Where? The citizen's house?'

Someone reminds regular customers who are starving:
Only available with coins, to-go with simple lunchboxes
Every time the window closes──a normal housing

-A Window-

XIII.

「我必須告訴你，深夜，千萬別到巷裡。」

一刃槍砲
劃破禮儀城鎮的巧靜，
留下門口守候的貓。

                                        -夜巷-

'Here is a thing. At midnight, do not go into the lanes.'

A blade of shooting
Slashed tranquility of the town with manners,
Left the waiting cat near the doorway

                                    -Night Lane-

XIV.

「到鳥岩，看巴士底夜景。」

你拿著星辰地圖給我看

低聲表達星座如何歡談。陣雨

鏡下——巴士底點燈的夜晚

-夜訪鳥岩-

'Go to Bird Rock for the night view of Basseterre.'

You showed me a map of the stars

And whispered about their happy conversation. Under the mirror

Of showers—— the night view of Basseterre

-Night visiting in Bird Rock-

西岸

Western Coast

XV.

舊路鎮；一座歷史小鎮；英國首個城鎮。英國的探險家——湯瑪斯 華納。聖湯瑪斯教堂，墓園裡的白亭。他定居、他見到、他導引——原住民的和樂、移民、戰爭、大悲劇、黑奴。

喔，探索者！歌頌孤帆裡的英國：
移民川流，島主的言笑之橋崩毀，
對於所忘，今日途人也無火。

-舊路鎮，白亭下-

Old Road Town; a historical town; the first British town here. The British explorer——Thomas Warner. In St. Thomas Anglican Church, under the white shelter in the cemetery. He resided, saw and lead——Aboriginals' happiness, immigrants, the war, the big tragedy, and slavery.

Oh, explorer! Singing for the sailing United Kingdom: The river of immigrants, the collapse of the bridge to islanders, Today, no person and fire for whatever are being forgotten.

-Old Road Town, under the White Shelter-

XVI.

硫磺山上沉睡的岩石巨人，

鐘和砲打持心跳，鳴動世仇繫的血。

頹圮老人！流連透視夢海的遊魂

-長眠的要塞-

The golem sleeping on Brimstone Hill,

Alarm and cannon make heartbeats and rumbled foes' blood.

The ruined elder! Phantoms on the coast roam still.

-Dormant Fortress-

XVII.

洋流奏起一段適宜的藍調⋯⋯
我們都將擁抱著沉重的名字死去，
天換天，慢魚也終將取代漂鳥。

-沉船臆想-

Currents perform suitable blues⋯⋯
We'll all embrace heavy names and pass away ultimately,
Day replaces day, slow fishes replace stray birds.

-Imagination for Shipwreck-

XVIII.

加勒比人語言：Liamuiga，是火山的名字，即肥沃的土地。

奔騰千年的火舌
今日的唇如此肥沃，住著
以影子為食的湖泊。

-火口湖-

The word of Caribs: Liamuiga, the name of the volcano, the

fertile land.

Tongue of lava had run for thousands of years
And its lips nowadays are fertile. The resident is
the lake feeding on passing shadows.

-The Crater Lake-

XIX.

雲霧繚繞的湖——Dos d'Âne Pond。

乘風輕沾水鏡，
浮雲是山的常客，
飄奏霧的卡農。

-湖之香頌-

The lake always with cloud and fog——Dos d'Âne Pond.

Touching the aquatic mirror by wind,

Floating clouds, as mounts' regular guests,

Perform the Canon of mist.

-Chanson of the Pond-

北岸
North Coast

XX.

史黛西亞對薩巴說：
「這廣藍慣了的海與天空
摻了點文明的雲霧與火」

-未褪色的藍-

Statia talks to Saba:

'The sea and sky is getting blue and wide

A few smog and fire of urban are blended'

-Fading Blue-

St. Eustatius & Saba

XXI.

面對面

浪片如白雪；雪白如片浪

言和的海；海的和言

-鏡像的海-

Face to face

Waves as white snow; snow white as waves

Seas of peace; peace of seas

-A Symmetric Sea-

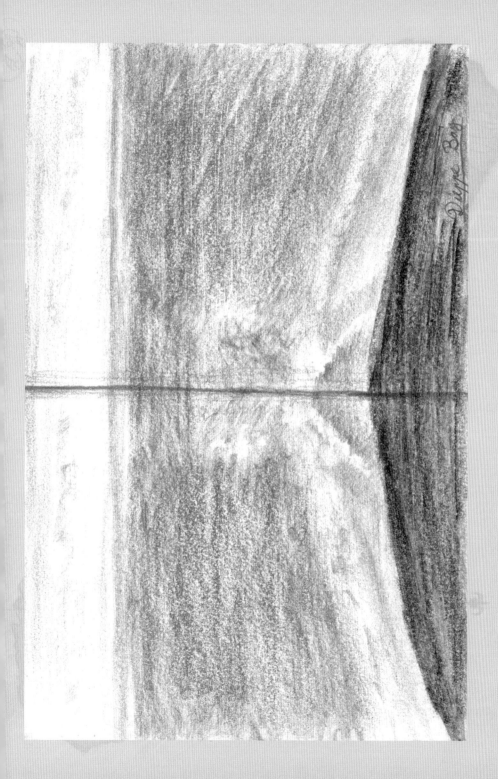

XXII.

海底的海綿礁，藏著珊瑚礁蟹。

在不斷變天的晴朗海底
習慣帶著夢鄉簽證的被褥
佯裝融入海綿的社會裡

                              -海綿礁的蟹-

Sponge reef under the seas hides coral crabs.

Under the sunny seas, an unstable climate

They used to take the bedding as the visa to dreamlands

And Pretend to get into the society of sponge

                              -Crabs in Sponge Reef-

XXIII.

「你想要去萊姆一下嗎？」
「萊姆？」
「就是，出去玩。」

平凡的人作為基酒。
為賦予靈魂滴入數滴萊姆，
而萊姆竟在萊姆之後。

-萊姆詩人-

'Would you like to go liming?'
'Liming?'
'That is to say, hanging out.'

Ordinary people as cocktail bases.
Drop a few lime to give their souls,
Then the lime is behind the other lime.

-Liming Poet-

XXIV.

火山噴發之後，風化留下黑砂，湛藍近海漂灰。

給我一幅家鄉的素描——
風景是取材自火山的海灘
怡逢退潮。

-對灰色的想念-

After the volcano eruption and the weathering, the black sand
has been left. Thus, the blue of coast has been dyed into the
gray.

Give me a sketch of my homeland——
The scenery could be the beach drawn from volcano,
And coincidently meet an ebb tide.

-Missing for the Gray-

東岸
Eastern Coast

XXV.

走向，東岸加拿大村，藍天，無雲，群羊啃食丘陵。

大地衣上的巴貝多綿羊
如拉鍊漫遊，那失焦的天空
著陸高崗，熨平草原之浪

-走向加拿大村-

'On the way to the Canada in the eastern coast, the blue sky,

no cloud, sheep are grazing on the hill.'

The Barbados sheep on clothes of terrain
Like roaming zippers, and the out-of-focus sky
Lands on a mount and irons waves on plain.

-On the Way to Canada-

XXVI.

東岸玄武岩岸——黑石。

熔岩及冷海之間
失控的火隨蒸氣遠離
復生之墨堆起的疙瘩山

-東岸墨詩-

The basalt coast on the east——Black Rock.

Between lava and sea,

The out-of-control fire left with steam

Revived ink piled the pimple mounts.

-Ink Poem on Eastern Coast-

XXVII.

遠離人群的一紙獨馬，
黑砂吸收蹄聲，被遺棄者的
嘆息，尚有海灣的容納。

-黑砂灣的騎士-

A paper of rider left crowded

Hoofbeat absorbed by black sand, the sigh

Of abandonees was embraced by the bay.

-Rider on Black Sand Bay-

XXVIII.

我走訪歐特莉 (Ottley's Plantation Inn) ──殖民時的莊園……

尋的跫音、訪的舊日莊園
海和雲、瞳與衣裳隨夕暈延燒
炙手雕琢字句裡的紅顏

                              -歐特莉的邂逅-

I've passed and visited Ottley's Plantation Inn──a manor of

the colonial age……

Footsteps being looked for, the old manor being visited

Sea and cloud, or pupils and clothes, both burn with sunset

With fiery carvings, I've noted the beauty within words

                              -A Seeing in Ottley-

東南半島
Southeast Peninsula

XXIX.

我們還能在此暢言
湛藍的母親給予孩子的家訓
在群山升起及日落之前

-亞特蘭提斯對孩子說-

Our talking here goes still.

Navy mother gives advice to her son

Before the rise of mounts and sunset

-Atlantic Says to Her Son-

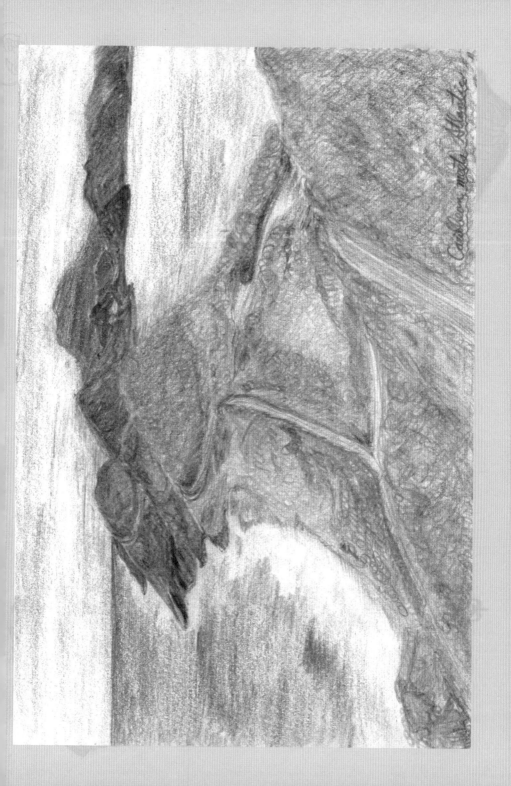

XXX.

海的臉上，無嘴歌唱。
面會遊魚、礁岩的苦訴
將祝福化作行走的浪

-風起漣漪-

On the face of the sea, no mouse to sing

Listening the complaints from fish and reef,

It translates from prayers into walking waves.

-Ripples by Wind-

XXXI.

「該如何稱呼她？」
「南洋櫻（<u>Gliricidia sepium</u>）。」

你的名字來自高海拔或溫帶
如今浸淫在熱帶島上花的群芳
仍是著你的名字做借代

-以櫻花之名-

'How to call the lady?'
'Mexican lilac (Gliricidia sepium).'

Your name is from mounts or the temperate zone
Overwhelming in the fragrance of tropical islands now,
I still replace the name with your name.

-Naming with Sakura-

XXXII.

聖彼得的山丘——猴山。

孤飛者離開明亮的港都
讓開闊的霧定義陸地的狹長：
與夢之商人同行的絲路

                                -猴山上的夢想家-

The hill in St. Peter——Monkey Hill.

Loner left the bright harbor

And let the wide mist define the length of terrain:

The silk road filled with the dream merchants

                                -A Dreamer on Monkey Hill-

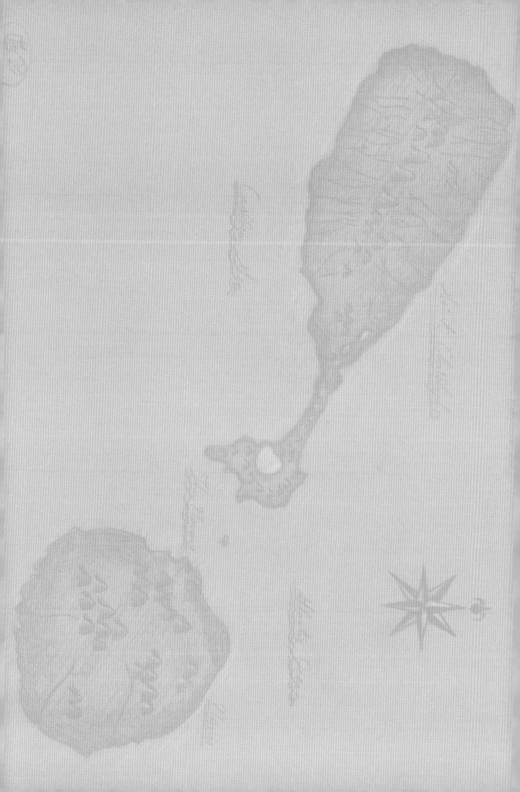

XXXIII.

在逐漸失明的白晝
別拒絕無盡延伸的海草原
年邁的海龜也曾經漂流

-老海龜-

During sight-losing days

Don't reject endless seagrass beds

Old turtles also used it to drift

-Old Turtles-

Turtle

XXXIV.

龍鍾的白蠶
高掛暗桑，飲繁星露
將夜編進海的綢緞

-月之舞-

The senior white-silk makers

On dark mulberry taste dews of star and sew

The night into the clothes of the sea

-Moondance-

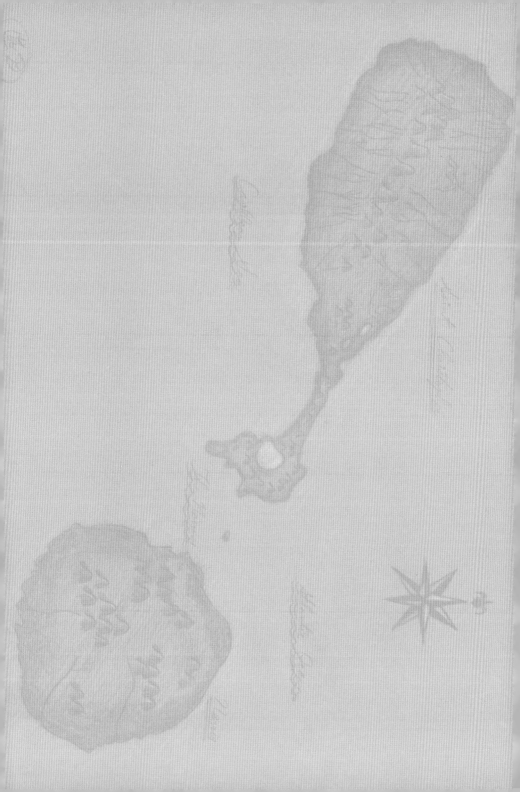

XXXV.

它長居於碼頭，而藍色血脈

隱晦地告訴它：風的家、洋流的故鄉

忘記淡水！從藍海行走到藍海之外

-大鹽湖的藍色孤兒-

The harbor it resides in, the blue blood it has

Self-hints: Home of winds, hometown of currents

Leave freshwater! From the sea to ocean

-The Blue Orphan in the Great Salt Pond-

XXXVI.

同是逐雨而居的兩座空城
一座人心層析；一座則為倒影
隨著懸於海上的河口移動

-落海虹霓-

The two empty cities both move with rainfall

One is the mental profile of mankind; the other is a reflection

Both of them move with the estuary above the sea

-Falling Rainbow Twin-

XXXVII.

相傳的文字會變質、會沉睡
同一處風景映入眾人眼廉
則會淌出多種色彩的淚

-賞景人-

Words will spoil or sleep as rumors
The same scenery within the different eyes
Will drip the tear with multiple colours

-Scenery Enjoyer-

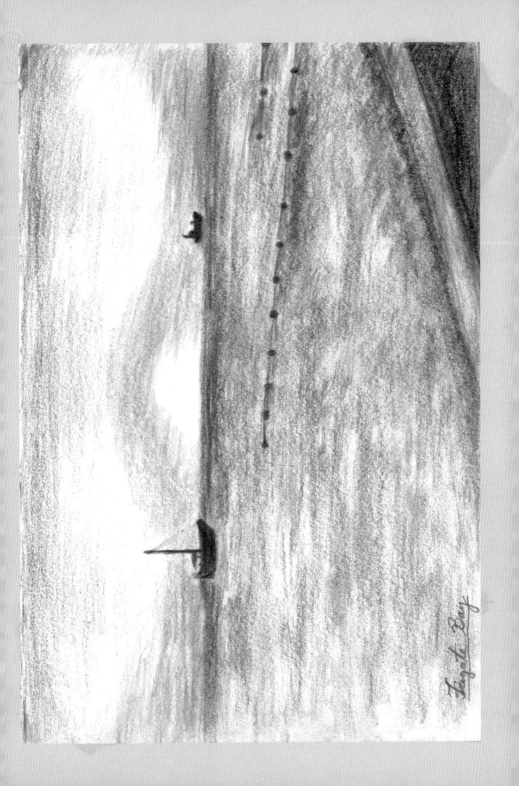

XXXVIII.

最南方，海龜　海灘，小型木造渡口。

我將情歌染進樁邊的綢緞
一人蹲坐賞景，以一點透視法
小船迂迴，水痕格外冶豔

-南方渡口-

The most southern place, a beach named Turtle Beach. There is a wooden pier.

I dyed the silk clothes near piles with love songs
A person crouch and enjoy the scenery with linear perspective
The traces of detouring boats are particular terrific

-Southern Pier-

XXXIX.

沙洲灣，每逢黃昏時刻，崖壁如同夕陽。

日子將晚霞的吻獻給石頭。
時間微風拂動你彤色的秀髮，
慢藍積攢自深海的壯遊。

-紅髮沙洲灣-

In Sand Bank Bay, every time dusk comes, the cliff here is just

like sunset.

Days leave kisses of glow to the rocks,

Breeze of time mollifies your redhead, slow blues

Are accumulated from ocean grand tours.

-Redhead Sand Bank Bay-

XL.

凱莉離開我活生生的相框。
金髮碎成沙；土耳其藍的眼睛
融化，緊貼著船隻們的故鄉。

-情陷快船灣-

Kelly left my living frame of photo.
The blonde weathers into sand; her turquoise pupils
Melted and adhered boats' home.

-Love in Frigate Bay-

XLI.

我棧宿糖糖灣，於夜晚賞星。
「是什麼蟲叫聲？」
「不是蟲，是吹口哨的蛙（Eleutherodactylus johnstonei）。」

海岸林間，群蛙低語、
模仿銀河說話的模樣，送吻信
給那位潛隱、明亮的醜小女

-糖糖灣的夜晚-

I stayed for a night in Sugar Bay, and watched the stars at
night.
'Where is the whistle from, which insect?'
'Not an insect actually, it's from the whistling frog
(Eleutherodactylus johnstonei).'

Frogs whisper in coastal forest,
Imitate the chatting of galaxy and send a letter kiss
To the ugly girls that are bright and latent.

-The Night in Sugar Bay-

納羅斯海峽
The Narrows

XLII.

聖基茨、尼維斯，彼此間的海峽：納羅斯。兩島間，靠渡輪來聯繫。

以兩島為畫架彼端，
裱框一幅名為納羅斯的黛色畫布。
輪機暈染──一筆癒合中的碧藍。

-海峽之橋-

The channel between St. Kitts and Nevis: The Narrows. The
connection between the islands depends on ferries.

The islands as the sides of an easel,
After framing a dark canvas named the Narrows.
It spreads with turbines──a recovering azure.

-Sea Bridge-

布比島

Booby Island

XLⅢ.

「你來自布比島嗎？」
「布比？布比島？」
「你，你笨拙　如島上的鰹鳥！」

衡量生命的驚奇，以漂鳥。
尋求劃破天際的、群聚海灣的，
唯有愚者忠於周旋無人的島。

-航向布比島-

'Are you from Booby Island?'
'Booby? Booby Island?'
You, you are stupid like booby on the island!'

To measure the miracle of lives with stray birds.
Besides the ones in several skies and coastal societies,
Only the fools still surround in the no-man's island.

-Sailing to Booby Island-

尼維斯
Nevis

XLIV.

「覆蓋著雪的島，我賦雪（Nieves）為其名！」哥倫布如是說
…………．
「那其實只是雲，永遠停駐的雲。」

白色戀人曾在我懷裡沉睡。
一首絕望的雨歌後，留下健忘的晴空。
仍愛著、戴著恬靜的你——雪帽融淚。

                                            -尼維斯的帽子-

'The island covered with snow, I give a name to her: Nieves!'
Said by Columbus.
…………

'That's actually cloud, a forever cloud.'

The white lover laid in my arms.
After a depressing rain song, a forgetful sky was left.
The tranquil you loved and wore still——a melting snow hat.

                                            -The Hat of Nevis-

※本作品曾登於蘋果日報20170401即時新聞

XLV.

「加勒比海女王——尼維斯。島上有處溫泉。」

啊，女王般的島嶼！
我化作舌尖，整理你液態的肌膚，
我臣服，閱讀你流動的火炬。

-小島溫泉-

'Speaking of the Queen of Caribbean——Nevis, there is a
spring in the island.'

Ah, the island named with queen!
My being an apex of tongue, cleaning your liquid skin,
I surrender, and` reading your flowing fire.

-Island Spring-

XLVI.

猶太人的墓園，墓碑上刻寫著三種語言：英文、葡文，還有希伯
來文。

失散的教徒
在荒島一處滴上
希伯來的石露。

-猶太秘途-

In the cemetery of Jewish, there are three languages on the
tomb: English, Portuguese and Hebrew.

Lost Jews
Dropped stone dews of Hebrew
On the barren island.

-A Secret Trail of Jews-

XLVII.

科特爾 教堂 已成一座廢墟。此地 仍存著 百年前的曙光：在
這裡，大家不分階級。

當花窗又再次焚燒，
舊日的人們自廢墟走來
在等高的長空裡祈禱。

-詠科特爾教堂-

Cottle Church has been a ruin, but, still, it's with dawn hundred

years ago: Herein, everyone is equal.

When the stained glass burns again,
People in time walk out from the ruin
And pray together on the same sky.

-Singing for Cottle Church-

XLVIII.

「聖基茨、尼維斯，復活節的假期，好一個禮拜五，想要放個風箏，為
何是陰雨天？而且連續三日，平日才又轉晴。」
「其實，貝里斯也這樣，很奇妙的現象。」
「確實！這昏暗的天空，我想起尼維斯　聖詹姆士教堂　黑色的耶穌像。
一樣，為何黑？為何總是雨天？都是謎。」

送群十字風箏到天邊
黑色耶穌藏於殘燭的教堂天空
受難後重生，泣作三個雨天

-復活節的雨-

'In the Easter vacation of St. Kitts, Nevis, I'd like to fly a kite.
However, why does rain come every Good Friday? Besides, there are
three raining days till our time to work.'
'Actually, the same as Belize. What an amazing phenomenon.'
'Indeed! And the dark sky reminds me of the black crucifix of St.
James Anglican Church in Nevis. The same, why black? Why always
rain? Both of them are puzzles.'

Let the cross kite to the side of the sky
Black Jesus is hidden in the sky of the church with dying candles
His resurrection from suffering, then tears, tri-day rain

-Easter Rain-

XLIX.

新生活，靛色躺椅。
擁抱再輕巧不過的藍天
放下習慣半百的重力。

-銀髮微笑-

New lives, indigo deckchairs.
We finally can embrace the lightest sky
And lay down the half-century gravity.

-Smiles from Elders-

L.

「你也來到此地？上一個　帝王，我忘了是誰。」
「帝王？閣下可舉例否？」
「比如說：美國開國元老、英國海軍將領。」

弄臣在此徜徉
唯獨書寫手稿
給過客的帝王

-受島的諫言-

'You come here also? The previous monarch…I forgot who he
or she is.'
'Monarch? Can you be more specific?'
'For instance, one of the leader of United States, the navy sir
of United Kingdom.'

Fools linger here
Write manuscripts only for
The passing monarchs

-Advices from the Island-

嘉年華
Carnival

LI.

當山崖崩塌
逐漸混入荒涼雨滴
直到旋律如泥巴

-土色民樂-

When cliff collapses
Soil gradually mixes with raindrops till
Its rhymes become a muddy place

-Muddy Folk Music-

LII.

展翅僵硬生活
飛羽劃破語言
斑斕爾後磅礡

-舞者-

Wings spread from boring life

Feathers here scratch languages

Colourful once and epic

-Dancer-

LIII.

祂從矮房漆色穩步而來
遠洋外的部落，再現眼前
熟睡者對七彩火焰的崇拜

-哨靈-

His steady walking from houses' colors
The tribes on the opposite of the ocean revive again
Sleepers' worshipping for the rainbow fire

-Moko Jumbie-

LIV.

年末的蜂鳥回憶：
在時間幾乎停止時，
才有最純的蜜。

-輕-

Humming birds recall this year:
At the juncture that time almost stop,
There is the purest honey.

-Light-

LV.

我們來跳舞吧，用交配舞慶祝！祖先們，受殖民者虐待，他們頻頻死去。我們，是延續的血脈，以此禮讚新生、新希望。

文明稀釋下
性愛列車各自上了軌道：禮儀至上、侵略、革命。
車站遺產喚作舞者之家

-交配舞半歌-

Let's dance, celebrate with mating dance! The ancestors tortured by colonizers and died one by one. We, with the survived blood, admire the relief with it.

Under the dilution of civilization,
Train of sex go on the trail: manners, invasion, revolution.
Heritage of Station is called as Home of Dancer.

-Half Song of Mating Dance-

LVI.

我再次遇見你，在嘉年華那時，我們曾經共舞。你、我，都有一處原始——二元對立彩繪，那時，我們無須言語，此時，我們擦身而過。

嘉年華時所妝點的二元對立圖
以兩個故事為粉底，補上了陌生的妝。
狂歡，被容許周旋於轉角後的第一步。

-轉角相遇的兩人-

I met you again, dear. During the Carnival, we were dancing together. Beyond you 'n' me, there is an origin——Binary graphing. In that juncture, we didn't need languages anymore. In contrast, this moment, we just passed through each other.

Binary graphs being masqueraded during Carnival
Makeup of strangers on the foundation with two stories.
Carnival, only allowed on the first step at the corner.

-Meeting at the Corner-

殖民九歌

Nine Songs for Colony

LVII.

此地，是聖地，也是死亡地帶。加勒比人聖河、英法的大屠殺，
兩千位原住民　血流三天三夜。

綠蕨與蘭花點上新生的顏色。
再訪那條斷頭又枯竭的歷史支流，
唯能細聆壁畫吐露赭紅的哀歌。

-三夜血河-

The place, not only a sacred place but also a dead zone. The
time saw the sacred river of Caribe, the pandemonium resulted
from British and French, the three-day bleeding from killed
aboriginals.

New colors decorated by ferns and orchids.
Visited the dry and beheaded river of time anew,
Bloody elegy only from the murals.

-Bloody River-

※本詩內文曾刊於國合會電子報165期「輕吟加勒比海的悲歌」，做為段
落標題

LVIII.

「你這住的小屋　可移動？」
「以前我的房子　不是屬於我的。解放後，我們雖有房子，土地
是莊主的，我們常遭驅趕。」

盼望回到上個下雨的帝國
暫居的島不過是棟意識的房子
為何慢？一具糖製的枷鎖

-非洲的蝸牛-

'The mini house you live can actually move?'
'In the past, my house was not mine. After the emancipation,
we had these houses though, the lands still belonged to the
manor owners. Therefore, we were often expelled during that
time.'

We wish we can go back to the last rainy empire
The temporary island is just the housing of awareness
Why slow? A shackle of sugar

-African Snail-

LIX.

「達爾文、華萊士，天擇說：適者存，不適者被淘汰。」
「在那個年代，到人類社會中——社會 達爾文的主義。」

在黑暗城下顫動的白色眼睛，
鞭子與刀下，他們失去了天擇。
取起沾血的骨牌許下祈願。

-來自暗室的呢喃-

'Darwin and Wallace. Natural Selection: Survival of the fittest.'
'In that time, it was brought into societies——Social
Darwinism.'

Shaking eyeballs in the dungeons,
Under leashes and blades, natural selection has gone.
They prayed with bloody dominos.

-Whispers from the Dungeons-

※本詩內文曾刊於國合會電子報165期「輕吟加勒比海的悲歌」，做為段
落標題

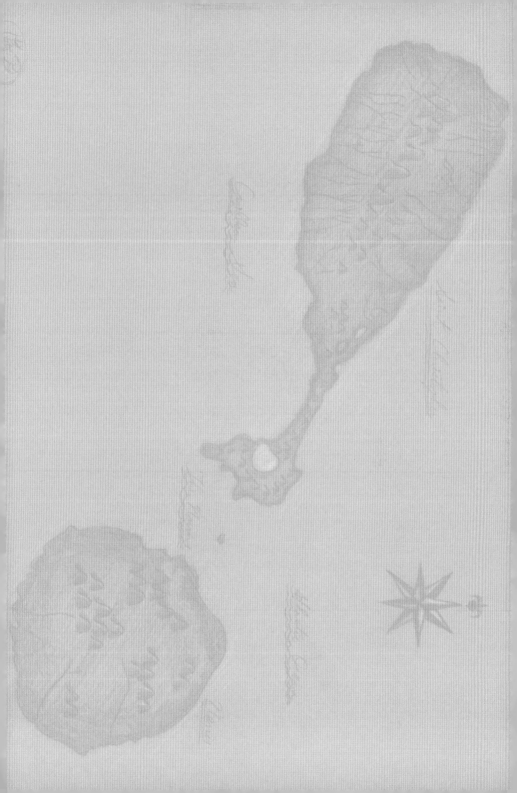

LX.

在早期，黑奴人力磨坊，手臂、身軀　易被絞進機器。以至於，
榨好的甘蔗汁　將被鮮血污染。此時，莊主下道命令：砍斷黑奴
手臂！別毀掉　我寶貴的蔗汁。

頹壞的遺跡低語著那段歲月：
「曾經的黑色霧氣本是黑色的肌膚。
時有脫離身體尋求自由的鮮血。」

-紅磨坊-

In the earlier time, slaves drove the mills by themselves. Their
arms, torsos were readily twisted into the machines, the
product, sugarcane juice, would be soiled with their blood.
Simultaneously, the manor owners would decide: Cut the arm!
Do not ruin my treasure.

The remains recall the age:
'In the past, black mist was actually black skins.
Blood looking for the freedom from torsos.'

-Red Mill-

LXI.

鹹魚。那時，英人捕獲鱈魚，並醃漬成鹹魚。送往聖基茨島，以此餵養黑奴，如今成為國菜。

昔日自遠方來的鱈魚肉碎
醃漬成鹹魚，近海的生魚
解放的今日該如何入味。

-從鹹魚到生魚-

Saltfish. In that time, schools of cod were captured by British
and pickled to saltfish. They were transported to St. Kitts,
being the food for slaves. Nowadays, it is a national dish.

Smashed cods in past from the distance,
Were pickled as salt fish, how to guide new flavor
From raw meat of coastal fish now.

-From Salty to Raw Fish-

※本詩內文曾刊於國合會電子報165期「輕吟加勒比海的悲歌」，做為段落標題

LXII.

擎天的煙囪是交易靈魂的殿堂

為殘疾的奴人裝上永動的齒輪

為天空城裡的莊主送上一匙糖

-失落的蒸氣國度-

Chimney to sky, palace for soul transaction

Perpetual motion being installed for disable slaves

A spoon of sugar to the owner of sky mansion

-A Lost Country of Steampunk-

LXIII.

巴緹克 (Caribelle Batik) ，一座古老莊園。這棵老雨豆樹，
由詩人 (Sue Mackiewicz) 所提及：它見證 四百年的光景。

告別沉重的土粒及石頭
枝椏跟著雲、海，也耐過颶風
繽紛的沉默高掛巴緹克山丘

                                        -老雨豆樹-

Caribelle Batik is an old manor. The old saman tree was

mentioned by a poet named Sue Mackiewicz: It saw the four

hundred years.

Farewell to heavy stone and soil particles,
Branches saw the passing clouds, seas and hurricane.
Colourful silence is hanged on the hill of Batik.

                                        -Old Saman Tree-

LXIV.

綠猴，殖民時期引進，有民眾會食用，將猴子肉稱為：樹棲 羔
羊。

牧羊人已經離岸
城鎮的、樹棲的羔羊群感慨
海是浪漫三百年的柵欄

                                    -被遺棄的羔羊-

Green monkey, imported during the colonial time. Some locals
like to eat and give a name to it: Tree mutton.

Shepherds have left already
The lambs from towns and forest all deeply sigh
Sea, the romantic fences over three-century period

                                    -Abandoned Lambs-

LXV.

耕田，我幻想　土壤的腐植質　自組裝——無外部干預下，物件
自行組織結構。

腐草下的土壤
礦物憑自我意識耕耘
無須武斷的鋤與太陽

-自組裝之歌-

During farming, I imagine the self-assembly of detritus in soil
——Without the inference outside, assembly can construct by
themselves.

Soil under detritus
Mineral plough with its own mind
Without strong hoe and sun

-Song of Self-assembly-

拉斯塔法里
RasTafari

LXVI.

拒吃加工食物、髒辮、大麻愛好者——拉斯塔法里教。

讓肉體飲入自然之血、
以鬍鬚、髮辮作枯藤，大麻
輕煙作靈魂——吹起不朽的視野。

-樹人-

Who rejects the artificial food, who wears dreadlocks, the

weed lover——Rasta.

Let our torso have the blood of nature,

Beard and dreads as faded ivy, marijuana

As soul—Immortal view they blow.

-Ents-

LXVII.

啊！流離的自然靈魂，

請安心住進為祢編造的辮子神殿，

自由的獅鬃行走於今日的巴比倫。

-恐懼之髮鎖-

Ah! The lingering soul of nature,

Please stay in the palace of dreads I prepare for you deity;

Lions' bristles are moving on Babylon now.

-Dreadlocks-

Dreadlocks

LXVIII.

錫安，泛指耶路撒冷 以色列。拉斯塔法里教，東非衣索比亞——
和平、自由、烏托邦。

從浮華客輪登陸孤島，
為自我及摯愛的人們
建起一座錫安的城堡。

-轉化-

Zion, or, in general, Jerusalem of Israel. For Rasta, it could be
Ethiopia in eastern Africa——a Utopia with peace and
freedom.

Landing from luxurious ships,
Building up a castle of Zion
For my loves and myself.

-Transforming-

LXIX.

雷鬼 教父 巴布 馬利 著名的一首歌：One Love。

島鏈上的人、靈魂與神聖
暫且擱置那嚴謹及詩的形式，
僅以簡單的日常用語讚頌。

                                        -世界一愛-

A well-known song from Bob Marley, the father of Reggae: One
Love.

Island people, souls and deities
Put the caution and form of poem aside,
Praise with colloquial words merely.

                                        -One Love-

LXX.

綠世界 假說：肉食、草食 動物平衡關係；防止植物走向 毀滅。
那些教徒內心 住著勇猛的獅——猶大族的雄獅 (Lion of
Judah) 。守護自己內心——那片無暇森林。

資本的臼牙、共產的慢性毒根
行走的草食動物、寧靜的綠色草葉
遵循法律的嚼食、八方團聚的雨林

-綠世界假說-

Green World Hypothesis: The balance between carnivore and
herbivore to prevent plants from going extinct. There are
brave lions in the minds of these believers——Lion of Judah.
Protect their own minds——The beautiful forest.

Molars of capitalism, toxic roots of socialism
Walking herbivores, tranquil and green leaves
legal masticating, reunited rainforest

-Green World Hypothesis-

群島之歌
The Song of West Indies

LXXI.

蟲民築城
群島喪血
大地鳴聲

-旱季短歌-

parasites' building

Islands' bleeding

Terrains' yelling

-Short Song of Dry Season-

LXXII.

美麗的島國──平衡的女人
逼婚的家族是來自異地的屠夫
婚禮，不見那鍾愛的男人

-枯心之島-

A beautiful island—A balanced woman

Forced marriage done with a family of a foreign butcher

In the wedding, there is no beloved man

-Island with Sorrow-

LXXIII.

偉大的旅行者：
你離鄉航行，仍帶著汲取神話的島嶼
群綠之日，文字成為失憶的歷史學者。

-致德里克·沃爾科特-

The greatest traveler:

You had trips with your epic island till the green day,

Words became the historians with amnesia.

-To Derek Walcott-

LXXIV.

　　那大航海時代，歐洲列強登陸 加勒比海諸島 及美洲，黑奴、殖民者、加勒比人、馬雅人，種族日趨複雜，誕生 魔幻寫實主義。

海盜的風暴隨貿易風行走，
落於煙島的、出生於煙斗大陸的
圖騰蝴蝶，揉合成不對稱的人偶。

-魔幻寫實引歌-

In the Discovery Age, Europeans landed on these Caribbean islands and the America. Slaves, colonizers, Caribs, Mayan, and so on. The complexity of race increased gradually, and, everlasting, the magic realism was born.

Storm of piracy floated with trade winds,
The totem butterflies on smoke or from pipe of tobacco,
Being merged into the asymmetric puppets.

-An Intro of Magic Realism-

LXXV.

古巴　莫希托：蘭姆酒、白砂糖、萊姆汁、薄荷葉。我　舉杯望著酒杯，正融化的冰塊，水分子在分散，熵增加——無止盡的混亂。

當你準備流浪，
做為譬喻，可以是熱帶的莫希托：
迷途的禮物是故事用的熵。

-對流浪的渴望-

Mojito from Cuba: Rum, white sugar, lime juice, and peppermint. When I look at my glass, I sense that there is melting ice. When the water molecules are scattering, the entropy increases——Endless chaos.

When you prepare to wander,
Metaphorically, it could be a glass of mojito in tropics:
A gift from straying is the entropy to write a story.

-Wanderlust-

※作品曾登於蘋果日報即時新聞；原詩名「旅行」於2018年校稿更為「對流浪的渴望」

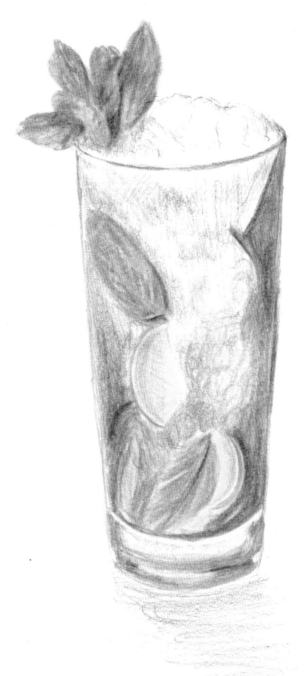

Mojito

LXXVI.

椰雲、白沙
溶進半朵夕陽
釀一杯仲夏

-鳳梨可樂達-

Coconut cloud, white sand

Melted with half of a sunset

Brew up a glass of summer

-Piña Colada-

Piña Colada

LXXVII.

紀念品店街上，寶石店，坦桑石——鐵達尼號電影　瑰麗海洋之
心。

我們可在海的囚禁中熟睡
卻盼比擬佩戴坦桑的蘿絲
跟隨思想的傑克遠走高飛

-大孩子的舶來品-

On the street of souvenir shops, the Tanzanite in the jewelry
shops——The gorgeous Heart of the Ocean from 'Titanic'.

We could sleep well within captivity of seas
But we all want to be the Rose with Tanzanite
And follow the Jack of dream far far away

-Imported Goods for Big Children-

LXXVIII.

聖三節　紀念三位一體（聖父、聖子、聖靈）之奧秘，主為羅馬公教、英國國教所守。

島上拜訪，奐奐教堂
遇見你時，正逢聖三節
奧妙恍若我對你的信仰

　　　　　　　　　-千里達般的女孩-

Trinity Sunday, to commemorate the mystery of Trinity, is mainly followed by Roman Catholic and Anglican.

Visited grand churches on islands
It was Trinity Sunday when I met you
Profoundness as my belief in you

　　　　　　　　　-A Trinidad-like Lady-

LXXIX.

騷莎舞，古巴 舞蹈，有拉丁舞的典雅，平民化、自由。初次與
舞伴接觸，步調截然不同，近一步，又退卻三分。

引舞人給彼此節奏
舊日散板的我有冷次的步伐
稍快板的你，調酒裡的電流

-給騷莎舞伴-

Salsa, a dance from Cuba, has the elegance of Latin dance,
suitability for civilians and freedom. At the first contact with
my dance partner, our tempos of us were totally different. I
wanna go further but back much more.

Leader gives tempo to each other
My Plague with the footsteps of Lenz's law
Your Allegro, the current in my cocktail

-To Salsa Partner-

LXXX.

相隔霓虹的內海
雪茄之煙，輕晃的吊橋
彼岸是詩的空白

-霧裡的精靈-

Between us, an enclosed sea of neon

The smoke of cigars, swing rope bridges

My opposite is the blanks of a poem

-Elf in Mist-

LXXXI.

古拉索（Curaçao），荷屬安地列斯（Netherlands Antillen） 之
一。嘟喜（Dushi），帕皮阿門托語（Papiamentu），甜美——
一切美好事物。

說起生命間的默契，
回溯到古拉索的財富：
純粹、甜美的空氣

-嘟喜-

Curaçao, an island of Netherlands Antillen. Dushi in Papiamentu
means sweet——All wonderful things.

Speaking of the chemistry among lives,
Let's go back to the treasure of Curaçao:
Pure and sweet atmosphere

-Dushi-

LXXXⅡ.

十四牖、一片心扉內
探頭者俯望那些進出的人類──
對稱的民房、歪斜的三百歲

-喬治時代-

In fourteen windows and a door of heart
Beholders look down on the passing people──
Symmetric housing, lopsided three centuries

-Georgian Era-

LXXXⅢ.

來走何方，不論身份
當地球儀上的釘刺逐漸失壓
敬那終將離開島嶼的島嶼人

-群島教我的事-

No matter who and where we are,

When the pressure of nails on globe gradually reduces

Toast with the islanders who finally leave the island

-The Tips from the Islands-

LXXXIV.

關於出生之地：
碎藍、碎土。乾與鹹的
那淚存在風裡

-仙人掌半歌-

About our place of birth:

Scattered blue or soil. Arid and salty

Tears are both in the wind

-Half Song of Cactus-

歌的碎段

Fragments of Songs

LXXXV.

火耕式的工作之後，
不受拘束地搭建一叢樂曲的篝火，
再拿啤酒做為這週末的湯頭！

-驚嘆島住民的生活-

After slash-and-burn works,
Bonfire of songs is built without any pressure;
Then, beer as the base of soup for this weekend!

-Daily life of the Islanders-

LXXXVI.

克國人　公車、計程車，車頭都有名字，常伴隨　電音、舞曲。

賦予名字之後
日子領她們從性感走向殘骸
舞曲是駐留心臟的電流

-當舊車高歌-

The Kittitians and Nevisians' buses and taxis all have their own
names. Besides, they are often with trance and dance music.

After naming,
Days lead them to go from sexy ladies to wreckages
Dance music is the staying current in their hearts

-When Old Cars Sing-

LXXXVII.

聖基茨，甘蔗火車軌道，大多軌道已廢，僅留 一段環島軌道——
觀光火車行駛。我乘坐火車時，想起 臺灣人的軼聞：為何我們
每人 都有英文名字？

我想呼叫你熾熱的芳名
你卻讓它上了訪客環島的軌道
真實的鐵軌持續濕冷

                                        -行駛中的假名-

In St. Kitts, there are the railroad trails for sugarcane trains
but majority are abandoned. Only, the round trail for the
running of tourism train. When I got on the train, I thought
something interesting about Taiwanese: Why does everyone
have English name?

I want to call your blazing name,
While you let it go on the trail for visitors
And make the one of reality damp still

                                        -Fake Name on the Way-

LXXXVIII.

島上的米有多種顏色，
那逍遙及忙碌的米相互笑著，
其它米已崇尚成為過客。

-一粒米看世界-

Colourful grains of rice on the island,

The free and busy ones mock each other,

others already tend to be passengers.

-Watch the world with Rice Grain-

LXXXIX.

「我和我來自東亞！」
擦身而過，一句鑲著國籍的問候。
我終將我埋葬於無名的樹下

-對東方浪人的寒暄-

'Me and I are from eastern Asia!'
A rapid meeting, a greeting with nations
I finally buried me under a nameless tree

-Greeting for an Oriental Wanderer-

XC.

熱情大蕉伴海螺肉，
溫帶的老饕客愛配著
用失語釀的蘭姆酒。

-細品餐後-

Plantain of passion with conch,

Temperate-zone gourmets love to order

With the rum brewed by silence.

-Detail after a Meal-

XCI.

當地盛行活動——健行（HASH），專走鄉間小徑。

讓我們離開主要的道路！
派出心靈斥候探索叢林小徑，
維持記憶疆土的牢固。

-健行的藝術-

The local famous activity——HASH, exploring the country
trails.

Let's have a jaunt from main roads!
Let our pioneers of psyche explore trails in jungle.
Then keep the stiffness of our memory lands.

-Art of HASH-

XCⅡ.

我們在想妄四竄的墓園裡嬉鬧。
承諾豈是笨重的石碑？俯視迷宮，
我愛你有如鴻毛，任海風輕飄。

-給情人的墓誌銘-

We frolic in the cemetery filled with desires.
Could promises be a heavy tomb? Look down the maze,
I love you as the feather floating windward.

-Epitaph for Valentine-

XCIII.

海綿礁上的苦旅：
用呼吸模仿面前的礁鯊，
彳亍在荒蕪的海城裡

-水猿-

Exhausting trips above sponge reefs:
We imitate the breathing as reef sharks,
Then linger in barren marine cities.

-Water Ape-

XCIV.

舞臺之上或卸妝之後，
持續地受到了社會的火焰灼燒──
藏著笑靨與淚的小丑

-人間默劇家-

Whether on stages or after removing make-up,

We are consistently burned with the flame of society──

Clowns who conceal smiles and tears.

-Mimes in Reality-

XCV.

酒吧裡的大麻氛香，
故事從太平洋日出說到長島冰茶
隔日，誰解我的醉、我落在誰的乳房？

-偷腥的貓-

Within atmosphere of marijuana in the bar,

The stories were gone from Pacific Sunrise to Long Island

After the day, what did sober me up, whose breast did I fall into?

-Who Is Having an Affair-

XCVI.

咖哩、咖啡
拉格、雷鬼
為思鄉流的淚

-東、西印度人-

Curry, coffee
Raga, Reggae
Tears from nostalgia

-East and West Indians-

XCVII.

我用一本本金箔
打造一座通往世界的天梯，
卻震顫、震顫地像火。

-從移民者那裡-

I use books of golden foil

to build a stairway to the world,

With quivering, quivering as flame.

-From Immigrants-

XCVIII.

貪婪的人居於詩的土地：

家庭、農村、城鎮、摩天大樓漸起，

仍伴隨著永恆的古老大氣。

-境遷-

Greedy people live in the land of poetries:

Family, country, city and skyscraper are built gradually,

With the everlasting atmosphere of age still.

-A Change-

返航
Return

XCIX.

都市給的遺忘藥
溶不進冰冷的螺湯。我的靈魂
絡繹航向加熱中的群島

                              -對群島的思念-

Forgetting pills that the city gave

Do not blend in lukewarm conch chowder. My soul

Consistently sails to the heating islands

                              -Craving for the Islands-

c.

醒來的我

行走在未來街道上，忘了

失去我，夢仍會繼續存活。

-歸與迴-

Awaken me

Walk on a future street though, I forgot that,

Without me, the dreams are alive still.

-Return and Linger-

CI.

那靈魂贊助者
贈我一張支票
做我們的資本

從支票到紙鈔
從紙鈔到銅板

是的
我們正做著
銅板生意

小額或大量的投資
於同貨幣的人群獲取利息
或前往不同貨幣的世界

難免地、漸漸地
彼此之間會有匯差

與那些滿足的靈魂晤談⋯⋯

行商的靈魂提及
「銅板的數大之美
卻是凌亂散碎」

流浪者的靈魂說道
「將銅板兌成紙鈔
甚至開張支票」

-金生金世-

The patron of souls
Donates us a check
To be our capitals

From a check to bills
Then from bills to coins

Yes, we are
We're doing the trade
With coins only

A few or scores of investments
We probably obtain interest from the same group
Or go to the world with another currency

Inevitably and gradually
Between us, there are the differences of exchange rate

The interviews with these satisfied souls:

Words mentioned by the souls of merchants:
'The coins, the law of large numbers
But the chaos still'

Words left by the souls of wanderers
'Changing, from coins to bills,
Even to checks'

                                        -Golden Life-

國家圖書館出版品預行編目（CIP）資料

航向驚嘆島 / 望海甘比 作.
-- 初版 .-- 臺北市：城邦印書館出版，2018.05
面； 公分
ISBN 978-957-8679-27-6（平裝）

851.486   107006939

航向驚嘆島 Sailing to the Islands of Exclamation

作者／望海甘比 Gambi and Seas

出版／城邦印書館股份有限公司

台北市中山區民生東路二段 141 號 B1

網址：http://www.inknet.com.tw/

讀者服務專線：（02）2500-2605

讀者服務信箱：service_inknet@hmg.com.tw

發行／聯合發行股份有限公司

新北市新店區寶橋路 235 巷 6 弄 6 號 4 樓

電話：（02）2917-8022　傳真：（02）2915-6275

初版／2018 年 5 月 10 日

ISBN ／ 978-957-8679-27-6

版次／初版一刷

定價／新台幣 360 元

本書如有缺頁、破損、倒裝，請寄回更換。

城邦印書館
cite E-printing　www.inknet.com.tw

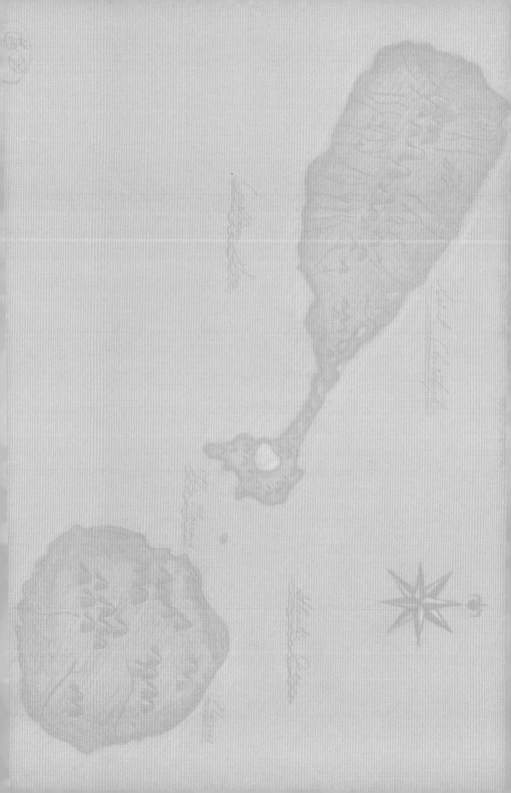